The mystery at Devils Tower
J

AR: 4.3
Pts: 2.0

DATE DUE

APR 2 1 2011			
AUG 1 2 2011			
APR 2 0 2012			
JUL - 2 2013			
JUL 1 3 2013			
JUN - 1 2015			
AUG - 2 2016		DISCARDED	

DEMCO 38-296

THE MYSTERY AT Devils Tower

Editor: Janice Baker
Assistant Editor: Susan Walworth
Cover Design: Vicki DeJoy
Content Design: Randolyn Friedlander

Gallopade International is introducing SAT words that kids need to know in each new book that we publish. The SAT words are bold in the story. Look for this special logo beside each word in the glossary. Happy Learning!

Gallopade is proud to be a member and supporter of these educational organizations and associations:

American Booksellers Association
American Library Association
International Reading Association
National Association for Gifted Children
The National School Supply and Equipment Association
The National Council for the Social Studies
Museum Store Association
Association of Partners for Public Lands
Association of Booksellers for Children
Association for the Study of African American Life and History
National Alliance of Black School Educators

Once upon a time…

You two really are characters, that's all I've got to say!

Yes you are! And, of course I choose you! But what should I write about?

 National Parks!

SCARY PLACES!

Famous Places!

FUN PLACES!

Disney World!

 New York City!

 Dracula's Castle

GRAND CANYON

On the *Mystery Girl* airplane ...

I can FLY us anywhere!

Mystery Girl

Or aboard the *Mimi!*

Mimi

Take me to the Forbidden City!

Or by surfboard, rickshaw, motorbike, camel ...

All great ideas! I can put a lot of history, MYSTERY, legend, lore, and LAUGHS in the books! We can use other boys and girls in the books. It will be educational and fun!

Good stuff!

Where will you get the other kids, Mimi?

From my Fan Club! Kids can apply to be characters!

And can you put some cool stuff online? Like a Book Club and a Scavenger Hunt and a Map so we can track our adventures?

Of course!

And can cousins Avery and Ella and Evan and some of our friends be in the books?

Of course!

Can I apply?

The *Mystery Girl* is all revved up—let's go!

You mean now?

LET'S GO!

*H*and so, Mimi, Papa, Christina, and Grant took off aboard the *Mystery Girl* and America's National Mystery Book Series—where the adventure is real and so are the characters! —was born.

START YOUR ADVENTURE TODAY!

READ THE BOOK!

GO ONLINE!

TRACK YOUR ADVENTURES!

APPLY TO BE A CHARACTER!

Yikes! That was close!

Rats!

1
CLOSE ENCOUNTER

Christina couldn't believe her eyes. The colorful disc hovered over the ground like a Frisbee. Strange, unworldly music poured from it and beckoned her closer. Christina spun on her heels, glancing in every direction. Her grandparents, Mimi and Papa, and her younger brother, Grant, were nowhere in sight.

I should run she thought. But Christina couldn't take her eyes off the beautiful disc.

The mysterious craft settled on the ground as lightly as a butterfly landing on a flower. Cotton candy pink, lime green, and aqua lights flashed and whirred around it like the gaudy rides Christina always rode at the Fayette County Fair back home in Georgia.

The lights danced faster and the eerie music grew louder. Christina watched in fear and fascination as the disc's side opened. Blinding white light poured from its belly and a spindly creature, not much taller than Grant, ambled forward.

Christina knew it was past time to run, but her legs wouldn't move. It was like she was jogging in a bowl of her favorite chocolate pudding. The creature crept closer. Christina's heart pounded. Bony fingers touched her arm. Christina screamed.

"*Whoa* there!" a deep voiced warned.

Christina's eyes popped open. She saw Papa's familiar cowboy hat above the seat in front of her. Beside him, her mystery-writing grandmother, Mimi, was typing away on her shiny silver laptop. The steady hum of Papa's little red and white plane, the *Mystery Girl*, had replaced the strange music from her dream. Everything was as it should be. Once again they were on their way to Devils Tower, Wyoming. Christina rubbed her blue eyes and stretched, thankful that she was no longer face to face with an extraterrestrial!

"That must have been some dream, Christina," Mimi said without looking up from her work.

"More like a nightmare!" Christina answered, still trying to clear the haunting images from her foggy brain.

"Well, maybe I shouldn't have let you watch that movie," Mimi said. "You always seem to have bad dreams after you watch strange movies."

The day before they departed for their adventure in Wyoming, Mimi rented a famous movie about Devils Tower—*Close Encounters of the Third Kind*. It was about a man drawn there to meet a UFO filled with friendly aliens. Christina had explained to her brother that UFO stands for Unidentified Flying Object.

Christina and Grant had traveled the world with Mimi and Papa while Mimi researched her mystery books. There weren't a lot of kids their age who had seen as many interesting places and met as many fascinating people as the two of them. And wherever they went, they had the uncanny ability to wind up smack dab in the middle of a mind-bending mystery. But they had never, ever, met any aliens!

Christina reassured her grandmother that renting the movie was a good idea. "You know I always like learning about the places we visit," she said. "I liked the scenes at Devils Tower. Now I know what to expect when we get there."

"That won't be much longer now," Papa assured them.

"Good!" Mimi said. She yanked off her red sparkly reading glasses and snapped her laptop shut. "The sun is getting low and you know I don't like to fly at night."

"I love to fly at night," Papa said. "That's the best time to see the pretty lights of the UFOs." He flashed Christina a mischievous smile.

"Oh, Papa," Christina said. "You know I don't really believe in all that UFO and alien stuff."

"*R-e-a-lly?*" a strange voice asked from the seat beside her. Christina watched the long, bony fingers from her dream peel back a blanket that she thought covered her sleeping brother. A shiny green head with bulging black eyes glared at her.

Christina screamed. Was she dreaming again?

"Grant!" Mimi scolded. "I told you not to use that get-up to scare your sister!"

"I should have known!" Christina yelled. She crossed her arms over her chest in relief. "Where did you get that?"

"Mimi bought it for me after we watched that UFO movie," he said. "Isn't it great? I'm gonna freak some people out at Devils Tower!"

"I think you'll freak them out worse if you take off the rubber head and show your real face!" Christina teased her brother.

"OK, you two!" Papa said. "If you want to get a good sunset view of Devils Tower, look out your window at 4 o'clock."

"But it's already past 4 o'clock," Grant complained.

"He means 4 o'clock the location, not 4 o'clock the time. That's what pilots say when they're talking about a position in the sky," Christina explained, pointing to the spot where the 4 would be on the face of a clock.

On the horizon, the Tower glowed an unearthly red in the sunset. It was beautiful, but bizarre.

"I thought it was gigantic," Grant said, disappointed. "I've seen anthills bigger than that!"

"We're still several miles away," Mimi said. "When we get closer, I promise you won't be disappointed."

"Uh oh," Papa said.

"What is it?" Mimi asked.

"We've got company," Papa answered. He turned in his seat for a better look.

Christina swiveled to see another aircraft gaining on the *Mystery Girl*. She pinched her arm, just to be sure this time. It hurt. This was definitely no dream!

2
UFO!

Christina watched Mimi's and Papa's concerned expressions and wondered if she should start believing in UFOs.

"The aliens are gaining on us, Papa!" Grant cautioned.

Suddenly a booming voice jarred their ears. "HEY THERE! THERE'S A NO-FLY ADVISORY ZONE CENTERED ON DEVILS TOWER. YOU NEED TO CHANGE COURSE!"

"Wow!" Grant exclaimed. "The aliens speak English!"

"I don't think those are aliens," Mimi said. She flipped on a reading light and studied Papa's map.

"If they're not aliens, then who are they?" Grant asked. "And why are they telling us there aren't any flies here?"

Mimi tapped their location on the map and explained. "No planes are allowed to fly over Devils Tower," she said. "That's why there's a 'no-fly' advisory. That pilot was doing us a favor by telling us."

"Oops!" Papa said. "Guess I was so excited about looking at Devils Tower, I wasn't being a good navigator."

Christina tried to help ease Papa's feelings. "We weren't close enough to smack into Devils Tower," she said. "I guess that's why they don't want planes flying anywhere near it."

"That's only one reason for the advisory," Mimi said. "President Theodore Roosevelt named Devils Tower our nation's first national monument in 1906. But for centuries it has been a sacred site to more than 20 different Native American tribes. Flying near it is considered disrespectful."

Christina noticed that Papa's eyebrows looked like kissing caterpillars. He always squeezed them together when he was concerned.

"Are we in big trouble, Mimi?" Christina asked.

"I sure hope not," Mimi answered. "I don't want to spend our vacation in jail."

"Well," Grant said, pulling on his rubber alien head, "I can't wait to see their faces when they slap handcuffs on a little green man!"

The tiny helicopter zoomed past Christina's window like a mosquito. The pilot made eye contact with her. He did not look happy.

At the airport, two men with orange-tipped flashlights waved the *Mystery Girl* to the corner of the tarmac. Christina recognized one of them as the helicopter pilot.

"I think I've got some 'splainin' to do," Papa said, killing the *Mystery Girl's* engine.

One man inspected the plane while the other pummeled Mimi and Papa with rapid-fire questions.

"Do you have a valid pilot's license?" he asked. "Did you file a flight plan? What is your business here? Why did you enter the no-fly advisory zone?"

When Papa had answered all his questions, the man seemed to relax. "I'm sorry to grill you folks," he said. "I'm John Ridge. I'm a park ranger at Devils Tower, although I'm off duty today. We've had some odd things going on around here, so I wanted to warn you about the no-fly advisory zone."

"Been seeing little green men?" Grant asked. He peeled off his disguise.

Ranger Ridge laughed. "Actually, I was afraid one of you might be another George Hopkins." He looked straight at Grant and winked. "You look like just the type to do such a thing."

Now, Grant was curious. He thrust his hands on his bony hips. "He must have been a brave and handsome explorer!"

Christina rolled her eyes. "Probably a little twerp," she said.

"Neither," Ranger Ridge answered. "But he was quite the daredevil."

"Did he dare the devil at Devils Tower?" Grant asked. "Sounds like a scary thing to do."

"Scary and foolish," Ranger Ridge said. "In 1941, he parachuted out of a small plane similar to your *Mystery Girl* and landed right on top of the Tower."

"Awesome!" Grant exclaimed. "Wish I'd thought of that."

"The only problem," Ranger Ridge continued, "was that he didn't have a good way to get down. He had a long rope, but claimed it landed in a spot he couldn't reach. Others say he chickened out when he realized how far it was to the ground. Either way, planes had to drop food and blankets to help him survive until his rescue seven days later. It was in all the papers and more than 7,000 people came to Devils Tower to see his predicament."

"How embarrassing!" Grant said. "So how'd he finally get down?"

"A brave college student led a group of rescuers up to guide him down," Ranger Ridge said.

Grant puffed out his chest. "The Tower didn't look that tall to me. I'm sure I could've come down on my own."

Mimi smiled and said, "Remember, you still haven't seen it up close."

"Will we get to see the top of Devils Tower?" Grant asked Ranger Ridge. "I'd like to know what's up there."

"There's only one legal way to get up there," he answered. "By climbing. And that's not something I'd recommend unless you're a very experienced mountain climber."

"Has a kid ever seen the top?" Christina asked.

Ranger Ridge's answer shocked Christina and Grant. " A 6-year-old boy and a 7-year-old girl have climbed the Tower."

"If little kids can do it," Grant said, "it should be a breeze for us!"

Mimi frowned and wagged her finger at Christina and Grant. Christina knew that

Mimi's wagging finger was like an exclamation point at the end of a sentence. "Don't you get any ideas," she cautioned.

The ranger inspecting the *Mystery Girl* ducked under the plane's nose. Christina noticed that his eyes were dark and serious—sort of like the eyes in Grant's alien mask. "Yes," he agreed with Mimi. "Curious kids can get into a lot of trouble around here."

Before Christina could ask what kinds of trouble they could get into, trouble found them.

ZOOOOOM! Something buzzed over their heads in a blur of colors. Christina dropped to the tarmac. Grant stared at the sky with his mouth open.

Christina's thoughts spun faster than a UFO. Ranger Ridge had said unusual things were going on. Now, she knew what he was talking about. They had an out-of-this-world mystery on their hands. She remembered her alien dream and shivered.

Will I meet my first alien on this trip? she wondered.

3
ALIEN VOICES

The peculiar light filled the air with electricity and a smell like sparklers on the Fourth of July. Christina's hair waved above her head like a wheat field on a windy day. Mimi's blonde bob was a frazzled mop.

Grant licked his fingers and combed his blonde curls. "What in the world was that?" he asked.

The rangers eyed each other nervously. "I'm sure it was just a ball of lightning," the dark-eyed ranger said. "Nothing to be concerned about."

But Christina didn't believe him. Even her brave Papa looked uneasy. "If there's a storm coming, we'd better hurry to our campground," he said.

Mimi, who hated camping, had wanted to stay at a hotel more than an hour away. "I don't want to sleep anywhere without hot, running water and an air conditioner," she had told Papa.

Always the cowboy at heart, Papa had wanted to "rough it" in the shadow of Devils Tower. He had told Mimi that nothing was more refreshing in summer than bathing in a cool river. "I'm a lady, not a fish," she answered matter-of-factly.

Papa rented a cozy camper as a compromise. Christina had been excited about staying so close to the Tower before she learned of the strange happenings. Now, she was nervous.

The camper rocked and swayed along the road to Devils Tower. Lightning crackled in the distance. It was the sharp, pointy kind that licked the darkness like a dragon's tongue—nothing like the colorful ball that had whizzed over their heads at the airport.

Grant watched the lightning too. He glanced at Christina. She could tell he was thinking the same thing.

"Looks like we've got a UFO mystery on our hands," Christina whispered.

"Yeah," Grant agreed, "an Unusual, Freaky, Out-of-This-World mystery!"

The campsite was pitch black. Only the occasional lightning bolt revealed the hulking shadow of Devils Tower. To Christina, it looked like an ancient, angry god.

"Who wants a fire-roasted hot dog?" Papa asked. He struck a match over the campfire. It sprang to life with a devilish glow. "We'd better get cookin' before it rains."

Christina's stomach growled. "Sign me up for two!" she said. She grabbed a forked stick off the ground that was just right for holding two hot dogs.

"Hey!" Grant whined. "Where's my stick?"

"Go find your own," Christina said.

Christina had already wolfed down her hot dogs and was roasting a third when something scratched at her neck.

"YIKES!!!" she yelped. She jerked her stick over her head to defend herself. Her hot dog sailed into the darkness like a missile.

Grant, who had poked her with his stick, fell to the ground in a fit of laughter. "Did you think an alien was tapping on your shoulder?" he managed to say between giggles.

"Not funny, Grant," Christina said. "That hot dog was cooked to perfection! Now you'd better find it!"

"Go find it yourself!" Grant said. "Unless you're afraid of the dark!"

"You're the one who'd better be afraid if I don't find my hot dog!" she warned.

Christina tiptoed to where she'd heard her hot dog land. She didn't want a hungry bear —or an alien—to find it and come looking for more!

CRAAAAK! A twig broke. Unless her hot dog had sprouted legs to escape, she was not alone. She held her breath and listened. Something sounded like humming insects. Christina soon recognized it as whispering voices. She strained to understand words like none she'd heard before.

"Did you find your dog?" Grant yelled. He marched her way with a flashlight. In its beam, Christina saw four eyes sparkling in the darkness. Tiny footsteps scampered into the brush.

Christina was frightened, but curious. Who or *what* had been watching them? She grabbed Grant's flashlight and motioned him to follow.

After a few steps, a squishy sound stopped Grant in his tracks. "Yuck!" he said. "I just stomped in poop."

Christina pointed the light at his foot. If there was poop to step in, Grant could always find it. This time it was worse. She glared in disgust as he peeled her squashed hot dog from the bottom of his sneaker and smacked his lips. "Yum!" he said. "It's still warm! Pass the mustard!"

"Grant!" Christina said. "Don't you dare eat that."

"You want it?" he asked.

"I'm not *that* hungry! Throw it away in the trash at camp!" she ordered.

As Grant turned to take the unfortunate hot dog back to camp, he noticed a jumble of footprints. Some were large boot prints with three dots in the center. On top of them were lighter prints, barely visible. Oval and without any markings, they didn't resemble any footprints Christina had ever seen.

"Do you think aliens could've kidnapped someone?" she whispered.

Christina expected Grant to dart to the camper and lock the door. She expected that she would be right behind him. But to her surprise, neither of them bolted. After all, how could they solve a mystery locked inside a camper?

"Let's look for more clues," Grant suggested.

A few steps later, a low-hanging branch snatched Christina's hair. When she untangled it, a long black and white feather tickled her hand. It had a red bead attached.

"Birds don't wear beads," she said.

Grant spied something white on the ground and snatched the light from Christina. "Birds don't have business cards, either," he added. "Looks like we've found our first clue."

One side of the card was too dirty to read, but the words on the back side were clear.

FIND THE WAY TO
BEAR'S LODGE—GO
TO TOWN—TWO
OVER FOUR DOWN.

4

DINOSAUR POOP

A cool breeze frolicked through the camper. It waved the aroma of frying eggs and bacon under Christina's nose like a waiter at a fancy restaurant. She stretched her long legs on the baby-bear-sized bed.

"Get your smelly foot out of my face!" Grant fussed from his cot.

"Well, why don't you get your smelly face away from my foot!" Christina said. "You need to **hustle**. We've got a mystery to solve."

"Are you sure we're still on Earth?" Grant asked. "Are you sure the aliens didn't kidnap us while we slept? I mean, this looks like a camper, but it could be a spaceship."

"Funny, Grant," Christina said. "I guess whatever we scared away last night didn't come back. Besides, unless those aliens stole her recipes, I smell Mimi's famous breakfast cooking."

Grant laughed at the thought of some weird-looking alien wearing Mimi's watermelon-red lipstick, red high heels, and red polka-dot apron.

Christina and Grant shuffled sleepily to the picnic table outside. Their dragging feet left dull snake tracks in the sparkling, dew-covered grass.

"Mornin' young'uns!" Papa said cheerfully. "Nothin' like eatin' your Mimi's breakfast in the wide-open spaces."

Mimi plopped steaming piles of eggs and bacon on the kids' plates. "Eat up! It takes a world of energy to explore Devils Tower!"

Focused on their mystery, Christina and Grant had forgotten what they had come to see. Grant scanned the horizon for his first look at the monolith.

"I told you it looked like an anthill!" he said. "I see ants crawling up the side of it." "Those aren't ants, Grant," Mimi explained. "Those are rock climbers."

Grant dashed back into the camper for a pair of binoculars. "You're right, Mimi!" he said. "Those little specks are people!"

Christina thought the Tower looked friendlier in the morning sunlight. "Do you mind if Grant and I go for a closer look?" she asked Mimi as she shoveled in her last forkful of eggs.

"As soon as you apologize for talking with your mouth full," Mimi said.

Christina gulped some orange juice to wash down the eggs. "Sorry, Mimi," she said.

"You and Grant can explore while Papa and I plan the rest of our day," Mimi said. "But don't go too far."

Papa agreed. "And remember," he cautioned, "this is not an amusement park. If you meet a snake or a bear, it won't be there to entertain you!"

Christina remembered the clue from the night before. But we've got to visit a bear's lodge, she thought.

After promising to be careful, Christina and Grant raced through the **vegetation** surrounding the campsite. They ended up in an open field that lay like a green welcome mat before Devils Tower.

Grant had expected the land to be dry and crunchy like a desert. But it looked more like a cow pasture. The enormous Devils Tower dominated a wide ring of Ponderosa pines around its base like a prehistoric playground bully.

The kids collapsed on the soft grass to study the Tower and several ant-sized climbers moving slowly up its sides.

"Do you know how tall it is?" Grant asked.

"I read that it's 867 feet," Christina answered. "That's taller than an 80-story skyscraper!"

Grant plopped on his side. "From this angle, it looks like a rhino horn with the tip broken off," he said.

They usually made a game of describing cloud shapes, but this time it was the Tower.

"See those deep grooves in the Tower's sides?" Christina asked.

"Yeah," Grant said. "It looks like there are columns between them like the ones on Mimi's and Papa's porch."

Christina's imagination was running wild. "I think those ridges look like Papa's corduroy chair," she said.

"Or the ridges in those potato chips I like!" Grant added. "How awesome would it be to have a potato chip the size of Devils Tower!"

"And an ocean of onion dip!" Christina agreed. She snapped her fingers when another thought popped in her mind. "Oh! It reminds me of the Play-Doh vase I made Mimi. I used your comb to make ridges down the side."

Grant chuckled. "So that's how I got green Play-Doh stuck in my hair!" he said.

"Got any more descriptions?" Christina asked.

"See that area near the top?" Grant asked. "The ridges look worn down and crusty. It looks like the scab I picked off my knee last week!"

"That's disgusting!" Christina said.

"OK, OK," Grant said. "I'll play nice. I think Devils Tower looks like an upside down ice cream cone."

"Much nicer than a scab," Christina said.

Grant replied, "No matter what, it's one weirdo of a mountain."

Christina sighed. "Don't tell me you didn't read ANYTHING about Devils Tower before we came," she said. "It's not a mountain. Some scientists believe it's the remains of an ancient volcano."

"Volcano?" Grant asked. "You mean it might blow?"

"No, Grant," Christina said. "They think Devils Tower was the lava that cooled and hardened inside the volcano in the days of dinosaurs. Sort of like those big plugs of wax you pull out of your ears!" she added. "Over millions of years, the mountain eroded and left only the lava standing. Other scientists think Devils Tower was just melted rock that cooled underground and was exposed after millions of years of erosion."

Only one part of Christina's explanation pricked Grant's interest. "So dinosaurs once walked around right where we're sitting?" Grant asked.

"That's right," Christina said. "Wyoming is famous for its dinosaur fossils."

"I'm glad they're gone," Grant said. "I wouldn't want to step in their giant poop!"

Christina's thoughts turned to their mystery. "Grant, do you still have that card you found?"

"Sure," he answered and wrestled it out of his pocket. Christina read the clue about Bear's Lodge again, and then licked her finger to rub the dirt off the other side of the card.

"Funny we're talking about dinosaurs," she said. "Here's a picture of one. This business card is for the Wyoming Dinosaur Center."

"What do aliens, dinosaurs, bears, and volcanoes have to do with one another?" Grant asked.

Before Christina could tell him she had no clue, a piercing cry shot across the open field like an arrow.

Is it animal or alien? Christina wondered.

5
ANIMAL OR ALIEN?

Grant and Christina cowered like cats in the grassy field.

"Shouldn't we run?" Grant whispered.

Christina shook her head and pressed her finger over her lips for Grant to be quiet. She knew it would be too difficult to outrun a bear or an alien's ray gun.

Another ear-piercing cry split the morning air. They could tell it came from a cluster of gray-green bushes that circled a tree on the other side of the field.

Grant quietly eased his binoculars up to his eyes. In a second he was laughing.

"Shhh," Christina cautioned.

"Are you afraid of a couple of birds?" Grant asked her as he stood up and brushed off the seat of his pants.

"Birds?" Christina asked.

Grant handed her the binoculars. "See for yourself," he said.

Christina aimed the binoculars and saw clusters of oily-black feathers with white tips flitting in the bushes.

"Got any salt?" Grant asked.

Christina could never understand how her brother's mind worked. This time she was really confused. "That's random, Grant," she said. "Why do you want salt?"

"Papa always says that if you can sprinkle salt on a bird's tail, you can catch him," he said.

Christina smiled. Papa had told her that same thing when noisy black crows covered their backyard in the fall. "I don't have salt," she said. "Maybe we can just sneak up on them. Follow me."

The kids crouched like lions in pursuit of an antelope. Slowly, they padded toward the bushes. As they got close, Christina noticed the birds had stopped moving. She held up a fist and mouthed silently to Grant, "On three." She slowly released three fingers, one at a time. When she raised the third, the two of them pounced into the bushes.

Christina didn't really expect to catch any birds. She expected them to fly away, startled. Instead, came yells of "OUCH!" "HELP!" "LET US GO!" They hadn't startled any birds. They had startled two kids!

"Sorry!" Grant said. He handed a Native American girl about his age the handful of feathers he had yanked from her long, raven braids.

"Me too!" Christina told the Native American boy she had tackled. Her face was redder than a stop sign when she realized she had ripped several pieces of fringe off his buckskin shirt.

The girl spoke first. "Grandfather will be disappointed," she said.

The boy looked embarrassed. "Ambushed by a couple of tourists," he said. "We'll never get our red feathers."

"What's so important about getting a red feather?" Grant asked.

"It means that we have mastered the ways of our ancestors," the girl answered shyly. "It means we know how to track game and find good water and defend our villages."

Christina felt awful that she had dashed their hopes, but she remembered her manners. "I'm Christina," she said. "And this is my brother Grant."

"My sister is Makawee," the boy replied, stone-faced. "And I am Takoda."

Grant was curious. "What do your names mean in English?" he asked.

"Makawee means 'generous,'" the girl answered.

The boy stood tall and puffed out his chest. It made him look even more like a statue. "Takoda means 'friend to everyone.'"

Christina wasn't so sure Takoda's parents had chosen the right name for their son. So far, he didn't seem eager to be *their* friend. He wore long braids like his sister and she noticed that the feathers he wore each had a red bead attached to them—like the one she found the night before. Had they been meeting with aliens? she wondered.

Grant had as many questions as Christina, but before he could ask them, Takoda said, "We have to return to Mato and tell him the bad news."

"Who is Mato?" Grant asked.

"Our grandfather," Takoda answered. "His name means 'bear.'"

Christina and Grant exchanged excited looks. Their only clue mentioned Bear's Lodge. If they could visit Mato's house, maybe they could find another clue!

6
SISTER-EATING BEAR

The sun had chased away the cool morning like a devil's pitchfork. Christina wished she had a colorful headband like the ones Makawee and Takoda wore to keep the sweat out of their eyes.

Christina and Grant had finally talked the Native American children into taking them to their grandfather's house. Christina regretted that she hadn't asked how far it was. She also regretted that Mimi and Papa didn't know where they were, just in case these children were leading them into a trap.

After splashing across a gurgling stream, they entered a wooded area with dappled shade. Christina spotted a boulder the same gray color as Devils Tower. "Could we take five?" she asked.

The kids plunked down on the smooth, cool stone. The Tower wasn't visible above the tree canopy, but Grant thought about the climbers in the boiling sun. "This is just the opposite of Devils Tower," he said. "Compared to this rock, we're giants. Compared to Devils Tower, we're insects. I like it better this way."

"I thought you wanted to see the top," Christina said.

"I do," Grant said. "But I'm afraid the only way I can climb it is if someone glues suction cups to my hands and feet—the kind a gecko has."

Makawee and Takoda whispered feverishly to each other. They weren't speaking English.

Christina felt sure they were speaking the same strange language she heard the night before in the brush near the campground. Grant wondered if it was the only foreign language he could speak. "Is that pig Latin?" he blurted.

Takoda looked offended. "Course not," he said. "It's the language of our people—the Lakota."

"I've never heard of the Lakota tribe," Grant said.

"We are part of the Sioux Nation," Makawee explained.

BOOM! BOOM! BOOM! A tribal beat echoed through the forest. "We must hurry," Takoda said. "The drums are calling us home."

Christina and Grant trotted behind Makawee and Takoda until they reached a clearing. A Native American village, complete with tepees, lay before them. "Wow!" Grant exclaimed. "It looks just like in the movies."

The drums pounded a steady beat and young men and women with painted faces danced in a large circle, sending little clouds of dust rising from their feet. Christina noticed that each of them had a red feather in their hair.

Makawee and Takoda led them to a tepee at the edge of the village. Paintings of cheerful yellow suns and grazing brown buffalo decorated the outside. But one painting sent shivers up Christina's back. It was Devils Tower with a gigantic bear clawing at its sides!

Takoda threw back the deerskin door. It slapped the side of the tepee like an enormous elephant flapping its ear. Christina's heart pounded in rhythm with the drums. She could see nothing. Takoda closed the flap behind them.

Inside the dark and smoky tepee, a small fire's dancing embers sent curls of smoke through a tiny opening at the top. When her eyes adjusted to the light, Christina could make out a face. It was ancient and leathery brown. A single braid pulled back hair as white as the smoke. Black eyes speared her with their gaze.

"Who do you bring?" the old man asked.

Takoda hung his head. "These children were able to capture us, Grandfather Mato," he said.

Christina saw that her friend was ashamed and tried to explain. "We were only playing," she said.   "We thought they were birds. "

"They have plenty of time to earn the red feather," Grandfather Mato replied. "They need more patience. Now, what do you want with me?"

"We found a card that mentioned your house, I mean tepee—the Bear's Lodge," Christina answered. "We wanted to see it."

"You've come to the wrong place," he said and motioned for Takoda to open the tepee flap. "The great Bear's Lodge is there."

Christina looked. "You mean Devils Tower?" she asked.

The old man's eyes grew angry. "That's the white man's name," he said. "Our people call it Mato Tipila. In your tongue, Bear's Lodge."

Grant was about to burst with questions. "Do bears live inside it?" he asked. "Christina said it was an old volcano."

Christina glared at Grant.

"Mato Tipila got its name from a story that's been passed down," Grandfather Mato said.

"Please tell us!" Christina begged. She plopped down on a colorful blanket, eager for the tale.

The old man slapped his palms on his buckskin pants. "A boy was playing with his sisters," he said. "The boy pretended to be a growling bear. The sisters pretended to be afraid since they knew their brother wouldn't harm them."

Grandfather Mato's eyes narrowed. "Then," he continued slowly, "the boy magically turned into a great bear."

Grant and Christina listened, wide-eyed. "Did he eat his sisters?" Grant asked.

"Listen," Grandfather cautioned. "The sisters ran to the top of a small hill to get away from the bear, but there was nowhere for them to hide. They prayed to the Great Spirit for help. Just before the bear reached them with his snarling teeth and slashing claws, the hill began to rise. The bear became angry and clawed the sides of the hill. But the hill rose higher and higher to keep the girls out of the great bear's reach. The bear's great claw marks are still seen on Mato Tipila."

"That's the painting on the outside of your tepee," Christina said.

The old man nodded to **acknowledge** her observation.

"So that's what made those gigantic ridges on the side," Grant said. He raked the air with his hands like they were claws. "That is so cool. Much better than Christina's volcano story!"

"But how did the girls get down?" Christina asked.

"Some legends say they were gathering flowers when the bear started chasing them," Grandfather Mato said. "They made ropes of their flowers to climb down."

Christina was still confused about the name. "Why did the whites call it Devils Tower?"

This time Takoda spoke. "I learned about this in school," he said. "Colonel Richard Dodge led an expedition to the Black Hills. When they visited this place, it is believed that his interpreter mistranslated the native language. He said the native people called it the Bad God's Tower. This was shortened to Devils Tower."

Christina thanked Grandfather Mato. "We should get back to our own grandparents," she said.

The old man stood slowly. "Remember," he warned. "The great bear can take many forms."

The warning gave Christina the creeps. Even strange lights in the sky? she wondered.

7
ONE MISSING MIMI

"You'd better watch out!" Grant warned Christina. "The way my stomach's growling, I might turn into a giant bear."

"I'm hungry, too," Christina agreed. "I sure hope Mimi's got something yummy for lunch!"

Christina and Grant had talked Makawee and Takoda into meeting Mimi and Papa and sharing a lunch. Christina didn't know if they would become good friends or not. But she still had so many questions to ask them.

"You two are so lucky to live in tepees in this beautiful place," Grant said. "Your lives are like a year-round camping trip!"

Takoda smiled for the first time since they'd met. "We don't live in tepees all the time," he said. "Usually we live in a house just like you!"

"Then what are you doing here?" Grant asked.

"Each year our people gather here from many places," Makawee answered. "Our grandfather comes all the way from his reservation in South Dakota."

"The legends say that our people were created in this area," Takoda continued. "It's a special time to pray and for the children to learn the ways of our ancestors."

"Do you dress like this all the time?" Grant asked as they arrived at their campsite.

"No," Takoda said. "In fact, I have a pair of sneakers just like the ones you're wearing."

Christina, who was bringing up the rear, looked at the children's feet. Their moccasins made soft footprints in the powder-fine dust. They were small, oval prints with no markings, just like the ones she thought aliens had made.

She pointed at the tracks and cupped her hand beside Grant's ear. "I think we've found our aliens," she whispered.

Christina could stand it no longer. It was now or never. She planted her hands on her hips and asked angrily, "Were you two spying on us last night?"

Takoda spun and faced Christina. "We hadn't planned to," he answered nervously. "We were following a man—practicing our tracking. When my hair caught on a limb, it hurt."

"If he hadn't yelped," Makawee said, "the man wouldn't have known we were following him. He wouldn't have run away."

"What was the man doing?" Christina asked. "Did you see what he looked like?"

"No," Takoda said. "It was too dark. We don't use flashlights when we're tracking someone."

"Have you seen anything else unusual?" Christina asked.

Makawee looked at her feet and squirmed. "I have," she admitted. "But Takoda doesn't believe me."

"What did you see?" Christina asked.

"It was a strange light," she said. "I was walking outside Grandfather's tepee a few nights ago and I saw it zoom over my head."

"We saw it, too!" Grant exclaimed. "We believe you!"

"Would you like to help us solve this mystery?" Christina asked.

"It might be a good way to earn our red feather," Takoda said.

Makawee clapped her hands in excitement. "We will help!" she said.

"Great!" Grant said. "Now can we pleeeeease eat?"

Christina called for her grandparents. "Mimiiiiiiii!" she yelled. There was no answer. "Papaaaaaa?" Still no answer.

"Maybe they're asleep inside the camper," Grant suggested.

Christina dashed into the camper. She was gone several minutes before she reappeared at the camper door. Her face was white. "Mimi and Papa have vanished!" she cried.

8
RIGHT ON THE NOSE!

Christina glared at Devils Tower and wondered if they had made a big mistake by coming here. The Tower had helped the Native American girls chased by the bear, but what help was it to them?

Grant was in a panic. He shook his fists in the air. "Just wait until I get my hands on those aliens," he said. "I'll teach them to take my Mimi and Papa!"

"Grant!" Christina shouted. "Calm down! Ranting and raving will not help us find any clues."

A blackbird landed in a pine tree over their heads and squawked loudly. When the kids turned to look at the bird, a sudden breeze rustled a piece of paper tacked to the tree.

"Look!" Grant said. He snatched the paper and read eagerly:

> *Dear Christina and Grant:*
> *You were late for lunch!*
> *We've walked to town. Hope*
> *to see you there!*
> *Love, Mimi and Papa*

"Whew!" Grant said. "Lucky break for those aliens!"

Christina gazed up at Devils Tower again. Had it sent the bird to help them find the note? But something still wasn't right. "It doesn't make sense," Christina said. "Why would Mimi and Papa walk 11 miles to town when they could've just driven the camper?"

"Yeah," Grant agreed. "And what would make them think we'd see them there?"

"I've got an idea," Takoda said. "Follow me!"

Takoda tore down the trail like a whirlwind. He was running so fast, his braids stood straight out behind him. The others struggled to keep up.

"If they gave a red feather for speed," Grant said between gulps of breath, "he'd have one already!"

When they finally stopped, Christina and Grant saw nothing special. The Tower loomed in the background, as it did everywhere in the park. Other than that, they saw only a grassy field dotted with mounds of dirt that looked almost like anthills.

"I thought you were showing us a shortcut to town," Christina complained. "You've led us to the middle of nowhere."

Grant, who was hot, tired, and still hungry, was also annoyed. "Where are the buildings?" he asked.

"Shhh!" Takoda said. "Watch."

The children stood motionless until they suddenly heard chirps and yappy barks that sounded like squeaky toys. Furry heads with pinned-back ears and beady eyes popped out of the ground like a furry crop of cabbages.

"How cute!" Christina exclaimed. "What are they?"

"Black-tailed prairie dogs," Takoda whispered. "Welcome to Prairie Dog Town!"

Soon the prairie dogs accepted their visitors and relaxed. Some munched on long weed stems. They reminded Christina of chubby little farmers chewing on straws. Others lounged beside their burrows in dirt that matched their sandy-brown fur. They might as well have been enjoying a day at the beach.

"Look!" Makawee pointed to three small prairie dogs. "The kids are playing chase."

"These holes and furry critters remind me of that Whac-A-Mole game," Grant observed. "I always win a prize when I play that."

Grant's comment set Christina's mind in motion. She climbed onto a tall stump, scanned the field full of prairie dog holes, and grinned. "I think I'm onto something," she said, and fished the clue card out of her pocket.

The others watched Christina stick her finger in the air and count. "One, two, over," she said. "One, two, three, four, down."

"What are you doing?" Grant asked.

"Remember our clue?" Christina asked. "It said, 'Go to town—two over and four down.' I know it's a long shot, but this is a town. I think you should go and check out that hole over there and see if there's a clue. But hurry up because we're not supposed to be near the prairie dogs!"

"Why me?" Grant asked.

"You said you always win a prize at Whac-A-Mole!" she answered.

The furry residents of Prairie Dog Town dove underground when Grant tiptoed to the hole Christina chose. He lay down on his belly and looked back at Christina. "I don't want to get too close," he said. "Something might bite me!"

"Just look and see if you can see anything," she said.

Grant eased closer and closer to the hole like a curious snake. He laid his cheek on the ground and peered inside.

"OWEEEEEEEE!" Grant hollered. He jumped and rubbed the end of his nose like it was on fire. "A prairie dog bit me right on the nose!"

Christina, Takoda, and Makawee laughed until their sides ached. When Christina could finally talk, she asked Grant, "Did you see anything?"

"Yeah!" he said with a frown. "Sharp prairie dog teeth!"

"Look!" Takoda shouted. He eased up to the hole, grabbed something lying next to it, and scampered back to the other kids. An angry prairie dog poked its head out and scolded Takoda like he was a kid who had raided the cookie jar.

"I'm glad I don't know what he's saying," Takoda said.

"What did you find?" Christina asked.

Slowly, Takoda opened his hand to reveal a small black canister. "Is this what you're looking for?" he asked.

"Wow!" Christina exclaimed, amazed that it had been so easy to find. She took the canister and was about to open it when someone sneezed behind them. She quickly stuffed the canister in her pocket.

Was the person who hid the clue watching them? she wondered.

9
PRAIRIE DOGS AND SECRET PASSAGES

"You kids enjoying the park?" a friendly voice asked.

The kids were afraid to turn around and look. Was this someone who was going to demand the canister from them? Someone who might even hand them over to the aliens?

"Is something wrong?" the voice asked. "Don't you kids remember me?"

Slowly, Christina and Grant turned. They were relieved. "Hello, Ranger Ridge," Grant said. "Why aren't you patrolling the skies in your helicopter?"

"There's plenty of work to do on the ground too, you know," he replied and rubbed his nose as if he were about to sneeze again. "These prairie dogs sure can stir up some dust."

"They're troublemakers all right," Grant agreed and rubbed his own sore nose. Ranger Ridge carried a heavy pick ax over his soldier. It was caked with red mud. Christina noticed that his boots were caked with mud too. "Have you been digging for gold?" Christina asked.

Ranger Ridge grinned. "Something like that," he said. "There are many things that are just about as valuable as gold."

Christina decided to impress the ranger with her knowledge. "I read about the Black Hills gold rush that happened in the 1880s," she said. "Since Devils Tower is in the Black Hills region, has anyone ever found gold here?"

The ranger lowered the pick ax to the ground and leaned on it like a cane. "Not that I know of," he answered.

Makawee spoke up. "The United States government gave the Black Hills to the Sioux people," she said. "When the white settlers found out there was gold there, the government took the land away from the Sioux."

"That doesn't sound fair!" Grant said.

"No, it doesn't!" Christina agreed.

"Many treaties were broken with our people," Takoda said. "It is sad, but we're all Americans now."

A familiar, deep voice followed by heavy footsteps brought an excited smile to Christina's face. "There you young'uns are! We had a feelin' you'd wind up here!"

"Papa! Mimi!" Christina cried. "Before we found your note, we thought aliens had nabbed you!"

"What would aliens want with a rusty old cowboy like me?" Papa asked.

"That's right," Mimi agreed. "I'm sure they'd bring us back in a hurry."

As happy as Grant was to see Mimi, he was even happier to see what she carried—a basket of food. "I've got a great idea," Grant exclaimed. "Let's have a picnic!"

"That's what we had in mind," Mimi said. "Introduce us to your friends and we'll find a spot to eat."

Grant quickly introduced Mimi and Papa to Makawee and Takoda and told them about their visit with Grandfather Mato.

"Would you like to join us, Ranger Ridge?" Mimi asked.

Ranger Ridge hoisted his pick ax back over his shoulder. "No thanks," he said. "I've still got lots of work to do!"

The picnickers settled under a tree where they could watch the prairie dogs play while they ate. "I wish I could take one home with me," Christina commented between bites of peanut butter and jelly sandwich.

She glanced at Grant. "A prairie dog would be perfect to guard my diary from a nosy little brother!"

Grant stuck out his tongue at his sister. It was stained purple from the grape soda he was drinking.

"With that yellow hair, red nose, and purple tongue, you are one colorful character," Christina said.

Makawee snickered. "It looks like you're on the war path!"

Mimi didn't know what caused Grant's red nose, but she was eager to join in the fun. "Yep," she said and laughed. "You need to get some sunscreen on that nose. You look like Rudolph the red-nosed reindeer and I haven't even started my Christmas shopping yet!"

Papa could see that Grant had enough of their jokes and turned their attention back to the prairie dogs. "Those are some controversial critters," he said. "Some people love 'em, and some people hate 'em."

"How could anyone hate something so adorable?" Christina asked.

"Once," Papa answered, "prairie dogs pretty much owned the prairies of the West. I read about a scientist who found a prairie dog town in Texas that covered 25,000 square miles and had about 400 million prairie dogs in it. But that was in the early 1900s. Ranchers felt that prairie dogs competed with their cattle for food. And horses sometimes stepped in their holes and broke their legs! So people shot and poisoned the prairie dogs to get rid of them. Today, most prairie dogs live in wildlife refuges and parks like this one."

"That's sad," Christina said. "But at least we know these prairie dogs are safe."

The kids ate until the picnic basket was picked as clean as a turkey carcass at Thanksgiving. Then, they stretched out on the grass.

"Why don't you open the canister?" Takoda asked.

"Mimi and Papa hate it when we get mixed up in mysteries," Christina whispered. "Let's wait until we're alone."

Grant nodded furiously. "If they had any idea we were involved in a mystery," he said, "they'd be worried. And if they were worried, they wouldn't let us out of their sight."

Takoda agreed it was best to wait. "How'd you like to hear another Sioux legend about the Tower?" he asked. "One about gold!"

"Are you kidding?" Grant asked. "Start talking."

Takoda sat up and crossed his legs—criss-cross applesauce, just like his grandfather sat when he told them the story of Mato Tipila. "Three Sioux braves went hunting," he began. "They were tracking a deer when they discovered a passage at the base of Mato Tipila. They made torches and went inside. They had to step over many human bones, but finally they came to an underground lake. The rock walls around the lake glittered with gold!"

Grant gasped. "Let's go and look for that passage!" he said.

"No, we already have one mystery to solve," Christina said.

Makawee agreed. "I want to find out what the strange lights are. Besides, I'm not sure I believe that story. I think Takoda made it up!"

"Did not!" Takoda said.

"Did so!"

"Did not!"

Christina was amused to see that Native American children argued just like she and Grant.

Mimi interrupted the argument. "You kids ready to head back to the campsite?" she asked.

"Can we explore just a little while longer?" Christina begged.

Grant poked out his bottom lip and showed Mimi his sad puppy-dog face. "We promise we won't be gone so long this time," he said.

Takoda had an idea. "Why don't you spend the night with us in our grandfather's tepee," he suggested. "I'm sure he won't mind."

"That would be awesome," Christina agreed. "And so educational, Mimi!"

"OK, I'm convinced," Mimi said. "Make sure it's all right with their grandfather, first. Then come to camp and let us know your plans."

"You kids stay together and watch out for each other," Papa called over his shoulder as they headed back to camp.

As soon as Papa's cowboy hat had shrunk to a speck in the distance, Christina plunged her hand into her pocket. She clutched the canister like a small treasure chest, gingerly shook it, and smiled. "There's something in there," she said, before cracking open the plastic lid and peeking inside.

"Interesting," Christina said.

10
SACRED SMOKE

"What is it?" Grant asked eagerly.

Christina used her fingers as pinchers to grasp the canister contents. She had expected to pull out a map or scrap of paper. Instead, she pulled out a tiny pipe. It was grayish white, the color of bone that had baked in the sun for years. Strange symbols covered its sides.

While Christina looked perplexed, Grant chuckled. "Don't those pesky prairie dogs know that smoking is bad for you?" he said.

Takoda admitted that the thought of a chubby prairie dog puffing on a pipe was funny. But Makawee was more serious. She examined the pipe closely. "It looks like a tiny version of a Native American peace pipe," she said. "But these symbols remind me of something else."

"Are you thinking what I'm thinking?" Christina asked.

"Only if you think these circles look like flying saucers," Makawee replied.

Christina thought back to the boot prints they had found on the ground their first night here. The circles on those boot prints looked like these circles!

"Maybe the aliens want to make peace with us," Grant suggested.

Christina blew out a long breath and let it vibrate her lips. It was a sure sign that she was frustrated. "You sound like a horse when you do that," Grant said.

Christina glared at Grant, narrowing her eyes. "It's just all so bizarre," she said.

Makawee was still turning the pipe over in her hands when she noticed that the end was loose. "Looks like this pipe is broken," she remarked.

"Let me see it," Christina said. She wiggled the pipe's mouthpiece until it dropped off into her hand. She tapped it on her palm until a small scrap of paper fell out. "There is more to this clue!" she cried. Drawn on the paper was a circle resting on three squares. A small "x" marked a spot on the circle. Another one marked a spot in one of the squares.

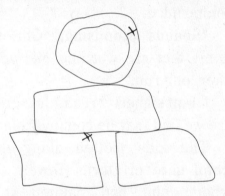

"Hmmm," Christina hummed. "Think. Here we have a pipe and a picture of a circle and some squares. What could it mean?"

"Maybe it's the instructions for blowing a smoke ring?" Grant suggested.

Takoda raised his eyebrows as if a light bulb had turned on inside his head. "Grant," he said, "you're a genius!"

"I am?" Grant said, dumbfounded.

"There's a huge sculpture of a smoke ring behind the prairie dog town," Takoda said. "It's called the Circle of Sacred Smoke. Didn't you see it when you got here?"

"It was dark when we got here," Grant answered.

Takoda leaped to his feet. "Follow me!" he commanded.

"Sounds promising," Christina said. "But my feet are warning me we're in for another long run."

Grant sighed. "Yeah," he agreed. "The smoke we find may be coming from my feet!"

The kids trotted along under the watchful gaze of Devils Tower. The late-afternoon sun had painted it a fiery orange-red. When they reached the Circle of Sacred Smoke, Christina was surprised to see that it wasn't a perfect circle. It looked like a puff of smoke from a peace pipe floating toward the Tower. A nearby plaque explained that the sculptor, Junkyu Muto, created it to promote world peace. He also wanted to show how much Devils Tower means to the Native Americans.

Christina was about to pull the clue out of her pocket when she noticed Makawee and Takoda's grandfather walking toward them. The tall, proud, old Native American in full Sioux garb licked a chocolate ice cream cone like a kid. It was an odd sight. They rushed over to ask if they could spend the night in his tepee. He kindly agreed and promised to stop by Mimi and Papa's camper to let them know.

After they said goodbye to Grandfather Mato, Grant begged, "Could we go in the Trading Post? I sure could use a drink. Mystery solving is thirsty work."

Christina was itching to investigate the Circle of Sacred Smoke, but she knew a drink would hit the spot for all of them. "OK, Grant," she said. "But don't get sidetracked."

Inside, the Trading Post dazzled Grant. The shelves overflowed with Devils Tower knick-knacks. Racks of T-shirts featured UFOs and little green men. Grant even found a green rubber alien head just like the one he already owned.

"What'll ya have, pardners?" the man at the snack bar asked.

Takoda plunked enough money on the counter for their drinks. "Sarsaparilla for all of us," he answered.

"Is that the stuff bartenders always serve to kids in the old Western movies?" Grant asked the man. "I've always wondered what that tastes like."

"It is," the man answered. "Best drink this side of the Mississippi River!"

Grant took a swig of the icy-cold drink and smacked his lips. "Mmmmmm," he said. "Tastes like root beer."

Christina agreed. "Excellent choice, Takoda!"

Refreshed, the kids skipped back to the smoke monument. With daylight fading, Christina quickly studied the "x" on the paper. She looked at the corresponding spot on the smoke ring sculpture. She was disappointed. "That's marking a spot in mid air."

"Yes," Makawee agreed. "But if you were a bird and followed the "x" you might just land in the Belle Fourche River."

"Let's see if we can find anything else," Christina said. The other "x" on the paper corresponded to a crack between the bottom left block and the top block that supported the sculpture. Christina ran her fingers along the crack until she felt a tiny scrap of paper that said:

FOLLOW THE
ANCIENT FOOTSTEPS

11
DOE OR FOE?

The sun sank smoothly below the horizon, like a slow-moving elevator. Immediately, the forest came to life. The park's bountiful birds had called it a day, but a toad, eager for music, cleared his deep voice and started to sing. Soon a multitude of crickets chirped in rhythm to his evening ballad.

"Should we be worried about bears?" Grant asked.

It was an open invitation Christina couldn't resist. "No," she said, "only the lions and tigers."

Almost on cue, footsteps crunched through the woods beside the trail.

"What was that?" Grant asked.

"No worries," Takoda said. "It's only a doe. You know, a female deer. I can tell by the sound of the steps."

After several more minutes of walking, Grant still heard the footsteps. "Are you sure that's a deer?" he asked. "It seems to be following us."

"It probably thinks it can get some treats from us," Makawee said. "People aren't supposed to feed the animals in the park, but it happens. Then, they become pests and have to be moved to other areas or even killed."

"The only creature I ever feed is Grant," Christina said. "No wonder he's such a pest."

"You are so funny," Grant said. "If you could see me, you'd know I'm making googly eyes at you."

"Too bad we don't have a flashlight," Christina said. "It's darker than a chalkboard out here."

"Well, maybe I should wish for some chalk!" Grant said. "Then I could draw a flashlight!"

The footsteps in the woods suddenly shifted into a flurry of feet dashing through the forest. "Wonder what scared it?" Christina asked. The words barely popped out of her mouth before a host of blinking lights surrounded them.

"UFO!" Grant screamed. "RUN!"

Grant took off like a jet on a slick runway. When the others finally caught up to him, he was perched on a stump just inside the Native American village. His eyes were the size of Mimi's china saucers and he was sucking air like a vacuum.

"Are you OK?" Christina asked, concerned.

"Didn't you see it?" Grant asked. "That UFO was attacking us!"

"Grant," Christina said calmly, trying her best not to laugh, "those were fireflies. If you hadn't taken off so fast, you'd have known that."

Christina glanced at Makawee and Takoda. She expected them to be giggling behind her. Instead they were staring at

Devils Tower. She followed their gaze, and thought she saw the glow of the rising moon. Then, she noticed colorful lights spinning around a large disc-shaped object. It circled the Tower slowly, then disappeared in a flash!

Grant tugged on his sister's shirttail and pointed at the blank sky where the object had been. "Christina," he said. "I may have made a mistake when I ran away in the woods. But *that* was no firefly!"

12

TERRIFYING TRACKS

Inside Grandfather Mato's tepee, Christina awoke to raindrops plopping on her forehead. She felt like a Chinese water torture victim.

In her sleep, she had wriggled off her pallet. Her head was next to the fire ring and under the opening in the top of the tepee. She cracked her eyes open just enough to see the dreary morning sky.

Sleep had not come easily. All four children had seen the unidentified flying object at the same time. Was it filled with aliens? When would it be back? What did it want? Their minds swirled with unanswered questions. Christina had tossed and turned long after the others had fallen asleep. She was good at solving mysteries, but was she good enough to solve this one?

After listening to Grandfather snore all night, or "saw logs," as Papa always said, Christina wondered how Native American families ever managed to sleep in one-room tepees. She moved her head away from the drips and listened. The rain pounded on the deer hide tepee like a drummer calling Native American braves to battle.

Finally, Makawee woke up. As soon as she heard the rain she looked at Christina and whispered, "What will we do? The clue said we had to find the ancient footsteps. How can we find them in the rain?"

"I've got an idea," Christina said. "Let's see if we can talk Mimi and Papa into taking us to the Wyoming Dinosaur Center. I don't know what it's got to do with anything, but it was on the card we found. Besides, it's always fun to learn about dinosaurs."

A piercing horn blast roused the boys and Grandfather Mato from their sleep. Grant was still unnerved from his close encounter from the night before. "What?" he asked and glanced wide-eyed around the tepee. "What is it?"

Christina crawled to the tepee door and peered outside. She could see their rented camper, which looked oddly out of place in a primitive campsite. Papa was sloshing toward the tepee. Rain poured off his cowboy hat like he had a faucet in his head.

"Good mornin'," he shouted to Christina when he saw her in the doorway. Papa ducked inside the tepee. Grandfather Mato stood. "Welcome!" he said.

Christina smiled. It was nice to see a cowboy and a Native American shake hands.

"Since it's too rainy to do anything else," Papa said, "We decided to take the young'uns to the dinosaur museum. Mind if your grandkids come along?"

"They will like that," Grandfather assured Papa.

Christina agreed. "Papa, you read my mind!"

"I'd better run to the bathroom first," Grant said. He turned in a circle. "By the way," he asked Grandfather, "where is the bathroom?"

Papa chuckled. "That would be outside, third bush on the left."

Grant looked puzzled. "Papa's just kidding," Christina said. "The bathroom is over there past the big tree."

Inside the camper, Mimi was waiting with breakfast treats. The kids munched on warm blueberry muffins and tossed juicy grapes into the air to catch them in their mouths.

Grant was telling Mimi all about what it was like to sleep in a tepee when he suddenly realized something. "Hey!" he said. "This camper is a lot like a tepee. We can take it with us wherever we go!"

"That's right," Takoda agreed. "When my people lived in tepees, they had to follow the buffalo herds that provided their food and clothing. When the buffalo herd moved, the people took down their tepees and moved with them."

None of the children talked about what they had seen the night before. And if Mimi and Papa had seen the flying disc, they certainly weren't saying anything about it either.

The museum was located in Thermopolis, a town famous for its hot springs. A friendly tour guide greeted them. "When people think of Wyoming," he said, "they think of cattle ranches and cowboys. Or maybe they think of wide open spaces where 'buffalo roam and the deer and the antelope play.'"

The guide continued like a parent telling a bedtime story, "But let me tell you—long, long ago, before the buffalo and the deer and the antelope, this is where dinosaurs roamed and played."

He explained the sad story of Wyoming's most famous dinosaur, an *Allosaurus* nicknamed "Big Al."

"When scientists found his bones in 1991, they could tell Al was a young dinosaur, but had many injuries," the guide said. "Al even had a sore toe! He lay down in a dry riverbed and died. His bones make up the most complete *Allosaurus* skeleton ever found."

"I bet that was worth a fortune!" Grant said.

The guide grinned. "Priceless," he said.

"Will we get to meet Al?" Christina asked.

"No," the guide answered. "His home is at the University of Wyoming. But we do have lots of other dinosaurs—even a *Tyrannosaurus rex* or two."

"*Aaaaaarrrrrrr!*" Grant demonstrated his best *T. rex* growl. Christina borrowed Mimi's camera and snapped a picture so she could show her brother later how silly he looked.

"I can't help myself," he said. "That's my favorite dinosaur."

The kids marveled at scads of dinosaurs that had lived on land and in water, and even saw an *Archaeopteryx*, a creature that many scientists call the first bird.

But the fossils that grabbed Christina's imagination did not have wings, sharp teeth, or scary claws. They were dinosaur footprints. She learned that a "trackway" is two or more footprints from a single dinosaur, and that many trackways were found in Wyoming, including some near Devils Tower.

She thought of their latest clue while she photographed the tracks. Then, she whispered to Grant, "Are those ancient footprints or what?"

When it was time to return to Devils Tower, Papa had already pulled the camper onto the highway when Christina yelled, "Stop!"

Mimi spun in her seat like something was on fire. "What is it?" she asked.

"Your camera!" Christina exclaimed. "I think I left it in the restroom."

Papa pulled back into the parking lot and ordered Christina to skedaddle inside.

"The museum is now closed," a voice announced over the loudspeaker, just as the door shut behind her. As she walked among the shadowy dinosaur skeletons, Christina felt a twinge of panic as the lights went off, one by one. Luckily, the camera was still perched on the bathroom counter where she left it.

On her way out, she passed an office. Christina knew it was rude to eavesdrop, but the conversation she overheard stopped her in her tracks.

"How much would those bones be worth?" a man's voice asked. Christina couldn't place it, but she had heard that voice before.

"If they were found in that location," the other voice answered, "they would be worth their weight in gold."

The office door slammed and footsteps headed her way. Christina's heart thumped like a scared rabbit. If she had heard something she wasn't supposed to hear, she was in big trouble. She high-tailed it to the front door and prayed it was still unlocked.

"Hey!" the familiar voice echoed down the hallway. "Wait up!"

Christina glanced over her shoulder. In the dim light, she recognized the dark-eyed ranger from the helicopter. Please, door, be open, she thought. Christina's prayers were answered. She dashed through the exit and dove into the camper. "Burn rubber, Papa!" she ordered.

Christina didn't tell the others what she had seen and heard. Maybe it was nothing. Still, her mind replayed the conversation. That ranger is up to no good, she thought.

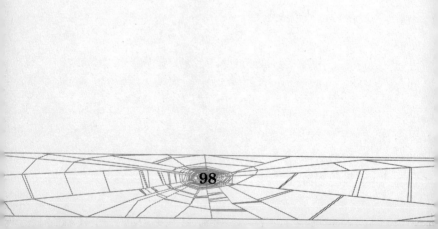

13
GIANT CHICKENS?

Takoda and Makawee spent the night in the camper with Christina and Grant. Takoda playfully called it Mimi and Papa's "tin tepee." Christina thought a better description was a rolling sardine can. But at least no UFOs disturbed their sleep.

The next morning after breakfast, Christina stuffed a backpack with snacks and useful items, including a flashlight. She wanted to be well prepared for a full day of clue hunting.

The hike to the river seemed endless in the scorching heat. Mimi had told them the Belle Fourche River had helped erode the soil away from the Tower long ago. But Christina couldn't imagine that when she saw it. The Belle Fourche rambled near the base of Devils Tower like a lazy snake. It was narrow and shallow and didn't seem to be in a hurry to get anything done.

When they reached the shady bank, Grant peeled off his shoes and socks. He plunged his toes into the refreshing water and sighed, "Aaaaahhhh. Have a nice, long swim, tootsie wootsies."

"You are so funny, Grant," Makawee said.

"After all the walking and running we've done in the past few days, my toe is sorer than Big Al's," Grant said. "There's nothing funny about that!"

"Yes, there is," Christina said. "Someday, someone will find your footprints in the mud of this riverbank and wonder, 'what kind of weird creature left these behind?'"

After they'd "cooled their heels," the kids resumed their search. They hadn't gone far when a tiny yellow flag caught Christina's eye. It waved from the top of a hill that the river had sliced open. The hill's red dirt was the color of an open wound.

"Follow me!" she shouted.

"Hey!" Grant yelled at the bottom of the hill. He rubbed his fingers over three-toed tracks. "Looks like a gigantic chicken's been walking around here. Makes me hungry for a Southern-fried drumstick."

"Those aren't chicken tracks," Christina said. "They're dinosaur tracks. Many of them walked on two legs like birds, remember?"

"Yeah," Grant said, "the kind that would swallow a kid in one gulp and lick his lips. Are you sure those footprints aren't fresh?"

"Look, Grant," she said, tapping the prints with her finger. "They're hard as stone."

"These must be the ancient footprints we're looking for," Takoda said.

"Gotta be," Christina said. "Let's follow them."

The kids scrambled up the hill. Soon, their shoes and moccasins were so caked with red mud, they could barely lift their feet. Each time they did, their shoes made a disgusting sound, like Grant drinking a thick milkshake through a tiny straw. Christina remembered how caked Ranger Ridge's boots were when they saw him at Prairie Dog Town and figured he must have been working in this area.

Just as Christina had suspected, the footprints ended abruptly near the yellow flag. She hadn't packed a shovel, but she dug into her backpack for the next best thing—a big spoon she'd taken from Mimi's picnic basket.

Christina stabbed at the gooey dirt until the spoon hit something with a dull clink. She scooped faster than Grant digging into a bowl of chocolate ice cream. "Got it!" she said.

Mud covered the small canister. "Let's wash it off in the river," Christina said.

"Let's wash ourselves off, too!" Grant said. "Last one in is a rotten dinosaur egg!"

Grant flopped on his belly and slid down the hill like an alligator. He splashed head first into the water. Takoda was right behind him.

"I won't risk losing this canister," Christina said. She carefully picked her way into the bubbling river.

Makawee agreed. "Boys!" she said. "I'll never understand them!"

Christina rinsed the canister in the river's gentle flow and dried it on her shirt before popping off the lid.   Inside was another clue!

FROM THE FALLEN GIANT GO ROUND AND ROUND. FIND THE YELLOW FLAG AND THEN IT'S FOUND.

14
RING AROUND THE ROCK

The kids hiked a trail through a jumble of boulders until they spotted one bigger than a school bus and twice as long. It was almost a perfect rectangle!

"That is one giant of a rock," Grant said.

"Sure is," Christina agreed. "And it looks like it fell off Devils Tower. This has to be the fallen giant we're looking for!"

Grant covered his head with his arms and stared at the Tower. "Maybe we should've worn hard hats," he said.

"There's nothing to worry about," Christina said. "Scientists believe the last big rock column fell off Devils Tower about 10,000 years ago."

The Tower looked so different up close, Christina thought. Now she couldn't see the entire shape, just the columned, vertical walls that stretched to the stunning blue Wyoming sky.

Grant studied the Tower's greenish tint. They hadn't noticed it from far away. "Why does the Tower look like it's been splattered with pistachio pudding?" he asked.

"That's lichen, a type of algae, growing on the rock," Christina said. "Can you imagine how much pistachio pudding it would take to paint Devils Tower?"

Christina leaned her head back until her chin pointed straight up, and watched a bald eagle soar over the Tower's edge. She understood why so many Native Americans felt this was a good place to meditate and pray.

Grant and Christina were surprised to see colorful cloths and ribbons tied to trees along the trail. "Looks like somebody forgot to take down the Christmas decorations," Grant said.

"Those are prayer cloths," Takoda explained. "Native Americans leave them as symbols of their prayers."

"Do you have Mimi's camera?" Grant asked Christina. "You should get a picture of them."

"No!" Makawee exclaimed. "To touch or take a picture of a prayer flag is like stealing a prayer."

Grants face glowed red. "I'm sorry. I still have a lot to learn about Native American culture," he said.

"It's OK, Grant," Makawee said. "At least you're trying."

"The clue said we're to follow yellow flags, but other than the prayer flags I haven't seen any," Christina said.

Takoda spotted the bus-sized rock again. "We've walked the mile-long loop around the Tower," he said. "Didn't the clue say to go 'round and 'round? Maybe we need to go around again, and look more carefully this time."

Christina had her doubts, but figured it was better to do it now than wait until dark. She passed out the last water bottles from her backpack and said, "Why don't we split up and see who can find a yellow flag first?" she suggested. "It will probably be like the one we found on the hill. We'll meet back here. On your mark, get set, GO!"

Takoda sprinted like a deer with Grant close on his heels. Christina and Makawee walked together, each concentrating on a different side of the trail.

Takoda was waiting at the bus rock when they finished the loop and found nothing. "Why isn't Grant with you?" he asked when the girls approached.

"What do you mean?" Christina asked. "Grant was ahead of us and we didn't pass him along the way."

Christina was worried. Had Grant disappeared?

15
CAPTURE THE FLAG

After 10 minutes passed, Christina became frantic. She thought about the dark-eyed ranger at the museum. She knew he had recognized her. She knew she had heard something important. Was he following them? Did he grab Grant off the trail?

Christina couldn't sit still any longer. "We've got to find him!" she said.

The kids galloped around the trail a third time. As they passed a Japanese family, Christina stopped. "Have you seen a boy with blond, curly hair walking alone?" she asked. The tourists only nodded and smiled. They didn't speak English.

Next, they met a sweaty rock climber with thick bundles of rope looped around his body. Oddly, he was running away from the Tower. Christina tried to ask if he'd seen Grant, but the climber didn't even slow down. "I just came down from the other side," he shouted. "I'd get away from here if I were you!"

Christina shivered. "What's going on?" she asked. "I wonder why that climber was in such a rush?"

Makawee gave Christina something better than an answer. "There's Grant!" she shouted.

Christina spied Grant high above the trail. He slowly picked his way through the boulder field that sloped up toward the Tower. "He'd better stop climbing right now!" Christina said.

"Grant!" Christina yelled. "Come down this instant!"

Grant kept climbing like a moth drawn to a flame.

"Maybe he can't hear you," Takoda said. "I'll go up and get him."

"No!" Christina said. "We're not separating again. We'll all climb up after him."

The children inched their way toward Grant over the treacherous rocks.

Occasionally, Christina yelled at Grant. When he finally heard her, he waved his hand over his shoulder and shouted, "Follow me!"

When Grant reached the boulder field's crest, he faced them and waved a tiny yellow flag in triumph like he'd won a game of capture the flag. But Christina's heart sank when he turned and disappeared behind a thick line of brush. "Just wait until I get my hands on him!" she mumbled.

Thunder rumbled a warning in the distance. "A storm is coming! Maybe that's why the climber told us to get out of here," Makawee said.

Takoda scrambled over the last few boulders and found solid footing. He reached back to help the girls.

"Thanks!" Christina said. "Now, help me find Grant so I can clobber him!"

They didn't have to look far. Grant popped out from behind a bush like a jack-in-the-box. "Boo!" he shouted. "You'll never believe this! I found the cave of gold!"

16
CLUELESS

"Never mind gold," Christina said. "What did you find near the yellow flag? Was there a clue?"

Grant looked sheepish. "I guess I was so excited about getting the flag, I didn't look for anything else," he said. "Besides, I heard something up here that drew me to the cave of gold!"

"What makes you think you've found gold?" Christina asked.

"Yeah," Makawee said. "I told you that's just an ancient tale. I don't believe it."

"Follow me," Grant said. He led them along the brush to the base of one of the many columns that formed the Tower. Up close,

Christina thought the Tower's columns looked like a bundle of gigantic sticks tied together for a bonfire. She only hoped it wasn't "their goose that was going to be cooked" on the fire! That was one of Mimi's favorite sayings. If your goose was "cooked," it meant you were in big trouble!

"This is the hard part," Grant cautioned. He shimmied onto a narrow ledge along the column.

"Now I know what Papa means when he says he's 'caught between a rock and a hard place,'" Christina said. She sucked in her stomach and held her breath as she moved next to Grant.

The kids found themselves packed onto a ledge with a small overhang above it. A strong smell of ammonia made it difficult to breathe. Christina heard a faint rustling sound.

"Makawee, can you reach in my backpack and pull out the flashlight?" Christina asked. "I'd get it myself, but there's not enough room to move."

The rustling sound grew louder and louder. "Let's get..." Christina stopped in mid-sentence. She aimed the flashlight above their heads.

"AAAAIIIIIIIEEEEEE!" The kids screamed as red eyes glared at them from the chamber ceiling.

17
NOWHERE BUT UP

Christina waved the flashlight wildly, turning the tiny space into a light show with dazzling beams leaping off the walls. "Run!" she shouted.

The kids popped off the tiny ledge like corks out of a bottle and gulped the fresh air.

"Were those alien eyes?" Grant asked.

"No," Christina replied. She rubbed her neck and quivered. "Those were bats!"

"Yuck!" Grant exclaimed. "So this gunk on the bottom of my shoes is bat poop!"

"That's right!" Christina said. "That's why the smell was so bad in there. I know that bat poop is used to make fertilizer, but I never knew it smelled that bad."

"We should have known," Takoda said calmly. "That's a perfect home for bats. Lots of birds make the Tower their home, too. Some parts of the Tower are even closed to climbers every year during the time that falcons are nesting."

"That's pretty cool," Christina said, "but let's remember we're solving a mystery. Grant, I need you to show me where you found that flag!"

Grant led them to a small mound of rocks beside a scraggly bush. Christina scratched the rocks away to uncover another small canister. She took a deep breath, and with trembling fingers opened the lid. "Let's see where this takes us," she said. This close to the Tower, she thought, the only place to go was up. As she read the clue, she realized she was right!

CLIMB THE LEANING TOWER. FOLLOW THE YELLOW CAMS TO THE TOP.

18

LEANING TOWER OF FEAR

"Anybody got bread and mayo?" Grant asked.

Christina looked puzzled. "Why do you ask?" she said.

"Well, I've never tried yellow ham, but it might make a good sandwich!" Grant replied, always thinking about food.

"Oh, Grant," Christina sighed. "The clue said yellow 'cams,' not hams."

"So what are cams?" Grant asked.

"Climbers put them in the cracks when they're climbing rocks," Christina replied. "They put their ropes through them to catch them if they fall."

Grant grinned. He knew all this from his YMCA rock climbing class but he liked keeping his expertise a secret from his sister.

Christina couldn't imagine climbing the Tower. She glanced at the sky. It was getting darker due to the coming storm. She'd read it took most climbers at least four hours to climb Devils Tower.

"Kids have climbed it before," she muttered to herself, "and I know how to do this. I learned climbing technique at Girl Scout camp last summer!"

"Everyone has to register to climb," Takoda said. He led the kids to the climbing kiosk in the visitor center parking lot. Then he headed to the "Leaning Tower."

Climbers often used the Leaning Tower as a starting point. Along the way, Takoda pointed out several climbing routes. "Look at that crack," he said. "That's where William Rogers put his ladder!"

"Who was William Rogers?" Grant asked.

Christina had read his story in one of her books about Devils Tower. "He was a local rancher," she said. "He and his friend William Ripley built a wooden ladder all the way to the top. In 1893, Rogers became the first person to reach the summit."

Christina thought about what she'd just said and continued, "There were probably Native Americans who climbed it long before that, though."

"I don't know," Makawee said. "But today, many Native Americans believe the Tower should be closed to climbers. They feel climbing is disrespectful, since it's such a spiritual place for Native Americans."

"Did you know," Takoda asked, "that out of respect for Native Americans, climbers are asked not to climb the Tower in June?"

Christina hadn't heard that before. "Oh," she said. "Why, oh why, didn't we come in June?"

Too soon for Christina, Takoda pointed to a humongous column. It looked like it had fallen asleep and leaned against its neighboring column for a nap. "There it is," he said. "That's the Leaning Tower."

"We'll do it together," Makawee said. She could see the worry on Christina's face.

"I can't let you do that," Christina replied. "Your people...it's disrespectful!"

"I'm going with you!" Grant said, "no matter what you say!"

Christina couldn't imagine what Mimi would say if she knew what they were up to. But she could imagine Papa's words: "Dag nabit, kids. Have you lost your cotton-pickin' minds?"

Reluctantly, Christina was about to help Grant buckle into a safety harness when a man ran toward them.

"Hey!" he shouted. "What are you kids up to?"

"He's caught us!" Christina cried.

"Who?" Grant asked.

"Remember the dark-eyed ranger from the airport?" she said. "I think he's the one who's been leaving clues!"

Takoda and Makawee didn't seem alarmed by the ranger's approach. And Christina couldn't believe her ears when she heard them yell, "Papa!"

"What?" Christina said, thinking she'd heard them wrong.

"This is our father, Little Bear," Makawee said proudly. "He's a ranger and a climbing instructor."

"What are you doing?" Little Bear asked. "Kids can't climb the Tower alone. It's a very dangerous thing, even for an experienced climber."

Christina was confused. She wasn't sure she could trust this man. After all, only a few minutes ago she had thought he was up to no good!

She looked at Takoda and Makawee. "You can trust our father," Takoda said. Christina told Little Bear about the clues.

"I've been investigating some things myself," he said. "I'll climb with you to the top of the Leaning Tower."

Christina was amazed that the same person she had been so suspicious of now seemed so **kind-hearted**. He offered climbing instructions as he helped the kids don their safety gear.

Christina took a deep breath to calm her nerves. Hand over hand, foot over foot, she started the climb behind Little Bear, listening carefully to his orders. Grant was right behind her. She pretended she was crawling over a big fat log that had fallen over a bubbling, shallow creek. The rock felt like fine sandpaper. Occasionally, her hand landed on a powdery-soft patch of lichen.

Climbing was the hardest work Christina had ever done—like a tough P.E. class that lasted the whole school day. Her muscles screamed, "Stop! We've had enough!"

When they'd made it about halfway up the Leaning Tower, Grant warned her. "Don't look down, Christina," he said.

Christina had mixed feelings. She was afraid to look down, but she also imagined it was a beautiful sight. Christina closed one eye and peeked below. The ground seemed to spin below her. She closed her eyes tightly until the **vertigo** passed.

When Christina peeked again, the valley spread out below her like a patchwork quilt waiting for a picnic. The Belle Fourche River was a rambling silver thread stitching it all together. She was still soaking in the view and filing it in her memory when she heard a whirring sound. A mountain climber was rappelling nearby. He had a wild look in his eyes.

"Are you crazy?" he shouted. "Get out of here while you still can!"

19
TRUST OR TRAP

Christina looked around, but could see nothing that would have frightened the climber out of his wits. There was still the occasional clap of thunder in the distance, but it wasn't close enough to be threatening—at least not yet.

The climber stopped suddenly when his rope became jammed in a crack. "Help!" he yelled. "It will be here soon!"

Christina was too afraid to ask what "it" was.

"Calm down, buddy," Little Bear said. "I'll come and help you as quickly as I can."

Little Bear was not in a good spot to leave the children and help the other climber.

"Let me get these kids to the top and I'll rappel back down to your position," he said.

Christina felt her stomach turn a flip. If Little Bear left them on top of Devils Tower and came back to help the climber they would be left alone as the sky got darker. She patted her backpack to make sure her flashlight was still there. It was. I should be in the camper playing a game of cards with Mimi instead of hanging on the side of this Tower, she thought. But Christina couldn't let Grant know how discouraged she felt.

She looked over her shoulder and yelled. "We're almost to the top of the Leaning Tower," she said. "Keep on goin'. You're doin' great."

Little Bear helped Christina reach a flat ledge just above her head. She used every ounce of strength in her body to pull herself to a sitting position. That's when Grant let out a bloodcurdling yell.

"Oh no!" he screamed. Something fluttered from a nearby ledge and nearly knocked Grant off the Leaning Tower.

"It was probably one of those falcons that Takoda was telling us about," Christina said, trying to sound calm.

Grant wasn't convinced. "Or a Native American spirit that's angry with us for climbing," he said with a trembling voice.

Little Bear reached down for Grant and yanked him up onto the ledge beside Christina. "We made it," Grant said. "We're at the top of the Leaning Tower!"

Christina rubbed a rock wall behind their heads that felt much rougher than what they had been climbing. It was a column that had broken off, probably thousands of years earlier.

"Ouch!" Christina whined when a jagged rock nicked her finger.

Little Bear pulled a Band-Aid from his first-aid pouch and covered the scratch. Then, he pulled out a small bag of powder. "You two need to dust your hands with this," he said.

"Is that the stuff gymnasts use?" Grant asked.

"Sure is," Little Bear answered. "It will keep your hands from slipping on the rocks."

Christina studied Little Bear's face. I hope I can trust him, Christina thought. But what if he's leading us into a trap?

20
ALIEN COPTER

Clouds were gathering, but the sun winked at them enough to keep the sweat running down their foreheads. Occasionally a breeze whispered in their ears, or an eagle's scream grabbed their attention like sharp talons. But mostly it was quiet except for the clank of metal clips. Each time Little Bear discovered a yellow cam in the rock, he threaded the rope through it and disconnected the one below him. "Always leave things exactly as you find them," he said.

High above their heads, Christina saw a bush that seemed to grow straight out of the rock. Little Bear told them that was the rim. Christina focused on that bush with all her might.

The darkening sky encouraged Christina to climb faster. She handed a granola bar to Grant, who was whining for a break. "Eat this and keep climbing," she said. Christina needed a break too. Her arms and legs felt like jelly.

Just when Christina felt she couldn't climb another inch, solid ground appeared before them!

"We're at the top of Devils Tower!" Grant shouted. Christina peeked over the edge. In the fading light, she could see two dark specks. "That must be Takoda and Makawee," she said and laughed. "Now, they're the ones who look like ants."

"I've got to go and help that stranded climber," Little Bear said. "Stay put and I'll be back soon."

When Little Bear sank out of sight, Christina swept the ground with her flashlight. Wheat-colored tufts of grass were scattered along the red dirt like hair on an old man's head. Nothing moved. Whoever or whatever was supposed to meet them was nowhere in sight.

Grant unbuckled his helmet and yanked it off his head. "I feel like we're on the moon," he whispered.

"Just be careful," Christina whispered back. She shined the light along the ground until the beam hit the edge of Devils Tower. "Remember this is only about the size of a football field. It would be easy to fall off!"

"What's next?" Grant asked.

"The clue didn't say," Christina answered. "Let's look around."

"Little Bear told us to stay put," Grant said.

"Well, he knows we can't go far," Christina said. "Besides, we might find what we're looking for."

The kids soon discovered the ground was slanting, like they were walking uphill. "I thought the top was flat," Grant said.

A sharp squeak drew their attention. Christina turned the light.

Shining black eyes met their stare and darted to a tuft of grass. "How in the world did that mouse get up here?" Christina asked.

"M-m-may-b-b-be the same way THAT got up here," Grant stuttered. The light illuminated a distant creature with a big head and skinny body.

Christina knew there was no place to run. "We might as well go and introduce ourselves," she said.

As the children inched their way forward, the creature didn't move. Just as Christina was wondering how to shake hands with an alien, they realized they'd made a big mistake. The "alien" was just a pile of rocks with a stick in the middle. The head was a big black canister.

"Whew," Christina sighed. "Let's open that canister." She expected to find a clue inside but was disappointed. "This is a list of names of all the people who've made it to the top of Devils Tower," she said.

"Hey, give me the pen out of your backpack," Grant said. "We can add our names to the list!"

Grant quickly scribbled their names, and was snapping the lid back on the canister when a whirling white light blinded them.

Rising above the edge of Devils Tower was the same UFO they'd seen from the Native American village. Only this time they were seeing it up close. "Wowwwwww," Christina said. "That's got to be what frightened those climbers."

In a minute, the outline of a man appeared against the blinding light. "What are you kids doing here?" a furious voice asked.

Christina quickly recognized the voice. It was Ranger Ridge! He laughed and said, "How'd you like to take a ride in my UFO now?"

"That's no UFO!" Grant shouted. He recognized the sound of whirring blades. "That's a helicopter with some kind of fancy lights on it."

Ranger Ridge laughed again and stomped toward them. "I'll bet when you saw it whizzing over Devils Tower it scared you, didn't it?" he asked.

When Christina saw his footprint in the red dirt, thoughts raced through her mind like race cars tearing across the finish line. His boot print had three perfect circles in it!

"That was you in the brush near our campsite!" she yelled. "You were the one planting clues. When we saw you at Prairie Dog Town, your boots were caked with mud and you said that some things were more valuable than gold. You were talking about dinosaur bones, weren't you? And if they were found on top of Devils Tower, they'd be worth a lot more than normal, wouldn't they?"

Grant caught on quickly. "You were creating UFOs to cover up your plan!" he added.

"You're pretty smart," Ranger Ridge said. "And if you pesky kids hadn't stolen the clues, I'd have buyers from the museum here right now! Those clues were for them!"

Ranger Ridge leaned closer to Christina and Grant when they heard someone behind them. Christina panicked. Ridge must have a partner, she thought.

"Stop right there, Ridge!" a voice ordered. It was Little Bear!

"I suspected you were up to no good, and it took these kids to help me get the proof I needed," Little Bear said. "The authorities are on their way. You'll go to jail, just for landing your helicopter on Devils Tower. When they convict you of trying to sell fake fossils, you'll be locked up for a long, long time."

21
RUNNING SCARED

Christina tapped her fingers in rhythm to the Native American drums. Grandfather Mato and a group of young men and women were performing traditional dances for tourists at the park amphitheater.

It felt good to be back on flat land with Mimi and Papa. It also felt good to have another mystery behind them. But Christina felt bad for thinking Little Bear had been the ranger up to no good.

She turned to Takoda and Makawee sitting beside her. "Why didn't you tell us your father was a ranger?" Christina asked.

"During this week we were living as our ancestors," Takoda explained. "We couldn't go running to our father—until our friends were in danger."

"You mean your father already knew we were planning to climb when he found us at the bottom of the Tower?" Christina asked.

"I saw him on the trail when we came out of the bat cave," Takoda said. "I signaled for him to follow."

Christina smiled. "I'm really glad you did."

Little Bear, who was sitting behind them, patted his son proudly on the back. "You kids did a great job of solving that mystery," he said. "Ranger Ridge wasn't even qualified to be a ranger. He lied on his application. When I started investigating, I learned he was making fake dinosaur bones. He also told people at the Dinosaur Center that he'd discovered fossils on top of Devils Tower."

"So that's what your conversation at the Dinosaur Center was all about," Christina said. "If you hadn't rescued us, we'd be fossils on top of Devils Tower!" Grant said.

Christina was about to apologize to Little Bear for thinking he was a bad guy when Grandfather Mato called Takoda and Makawee to the stage.

"I am proud to name the newest members of our tribe," Grandfather said. He placed red feathers in Takoda's and Makawee's hair. Christina and Grant clapped proudly. But they were not prepared for what happened next!

Grandfather Mato called Christina and Grant to the stage. "I am also proud to name two honorary members to our tribe," he said. He placed a red feather in Christina's hair and gave her the Native American name Washta. "It means 'good,'" he explained. "You are good at solving clues."

Grandfather then stuck a red feather in Grant's hair. "I will call you Chayton," he said. "It means 'falcon.' You went where the falcon lives."

After the ceremony, the kids said goodbye and promised to visit. "But next time," Christina said, "I want to visit in June when there's no climbing allowed!"

On the way home in the *Mystery Girl*, Mimi and Papa gave the kids the worst tongue lashing of their lives for climbing Devils Tower. After she had made her point, Mimi decided to change the subject. "How do you two like your Native American names?" she asked.

"Mine's cool," Grant said. "But I thought Grandfather would call me something like Running Bear."

Christina laughed. "Remember that close encounter you had with fireflies?" she asked. "I think Grandfather should have named you Running Scared!"

"Ha ha ha," Grant replied. "I just thought of something. The UFO that whizzed over our heads that first night at the airport couldn't have been a helicopter. What do you think it was?"

Christina pulled on Grant's shiny green alien head and answered in a deep voice, "Some things will always remain a mystery, my brother!"

Well, that was fun!

Wow, glad we solved that mystery!

Where shall we go next?

EVERYWHERE!

The End

Now...go to
www.carolemarshmysteries.com
and...

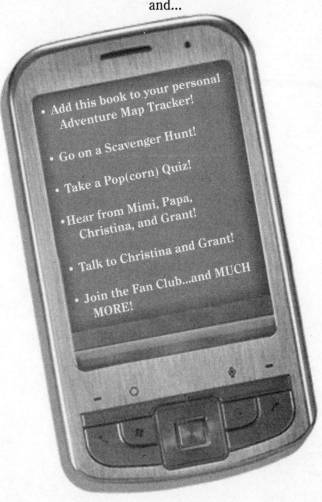

- Add this book to your personal Adventure Map Tracker!

- Go on a Scavenger Hunt!

- Take a Pop(corn) Quiz!

- Hear from Mimi, Papa, Christina, and Grant!

- Talk to Christina and Grant!

- Join the Fan Club...and MUCH MORE!

GLOSSARY

alien: a being from another planet

compromise: when two or more sides agree to accept less than they originally wanted

extraterrestrial: a living being that comes from outside Earth

gaudy: brightly colored or showily decorated

monument: a site preserved for its historical, cultural, or aesthetic importance; a large stone statue or carving designed as a tribute to a person, group of people, or an event

predicament: a difficult, unpleasant, or embarrassing situation from which there is no clear or easy way out

treacherous: involving hidden dangers

SAT GLOSSARY

acknowledge: to recognize or show awareness of something

hustle: to hurry

kind-hearted: showing courtesy or caring about somebody

vegetation: plants in general or the mass of plants growing in a particular place

vertigo: dizziness